# BAMZ

## AND THE CASE OF THE BULLIES

Stand up to bullying!

Enjoy the adventure!

Shazida

**SHAZIDA AHMED**

First published in the UK in 2023
by Lion Hill Publishing

Text © Shazida Ahmed 2022

Cover and inside illustrations © Aisha Haider 2022

A CIP catalogue record for this book is available from the British Library

ISBN 978 1 7392336 0 0

Printed and bound in Great Britain by IngramSpark

*Bully, Bully, go away*

*Don't come back another day*

*We stand united against your wicked ways*

*Say no to bullying*

*In every way*

# CONTENTS

# Chapter One

## *ADAM*

**Hi, I'm Adam.** I'm nine years old and I live at 88 Apple Custard Avenue. I know! Whoever named a street after my favourite pie was just awesome!

I have one brother Jamal, who is two, and even though he's a pain, it could be worse. Jamal could be crying all the time, instead, he is usually laughing or trying to talk. He sounds very much like squeaky mouses. Oops, I mean *mice*. If it's one, it's a mouse, but more than one, makes mice. My dad taught me that, or was it my teacher, Mrs Banshee? I always forget. So, this is my family - me, my mum, my dad, and my baby brother. My Grandpa Ali, and Grandma Yasmin are also in my family, but they live far away, so I only get to see them on school holidays.

## Chapter Two

# LION HILL

**Let me tell you** about my school, Lion Hill. It sits on a hill, and some say they once saw a lion lurking nearby and that is how it got its name, but I haven't seen one yet. I like going to school. I have lots of friends there and the teachers are cool. Well, some of them are.

We also get to do some fun activities, like the football tournament that happens every summer and we get to celebrate all the different occasions such as Christmas, Eid, Hanukkah and Diwali. My favourite teacher is Mrs Oppodopolus. She has a cool name. It sounds like a type of dinosaur! Mrs Oppodopolus lets me draw

and paint and make anything I want. The worst teacher in the whole wide world is our science teacher Mr Shivers. I don't like him because he never lets me do any experiments. He says it's because last time I burnt Sarah's hair, but it wasn't my fault. She put her hair in the way of my experiment and it got burnt!

## Chapter Three

# BILLY, MILLY AND ZACK

**My best friends** at school are Billy, Milly and Zack. Milly loves to take pictures. She has a camera that she uses to take pictures of everything and everyone. She also likes playing football with us all and is sometimes the bossy one in the group as she is always telling us all what to do. Zack is the clever one - he came top in Maths last year. He also likes to plan things and always has a plan in action when we have something to do. Billy likes to tell jokes, loves chocolate and is good at climbing up things. Last week, he climbed up the school gate and wouldn't come down until we'd listened to ten of his jokes. To be honest, Billy's jokes are *terrible*!

Get down! You'll be in trouble!

13

That day, Billy had just finished telling us a joke when Mr Shivers came outside and spotted him on top of the gate. He was not happy, and even though the rest of us hadn't done anything wrong, we had to work in the library, making sure all the books were in alphabetical order, and that was during break time!! I don't think Billy will ever climb up a school gate again, or if he does, we'll leave him to it. He said he owed us all a chocolate bar each, but that was a week ago, so I think he must have eaten them all on his own.

Then there's me. I'm good at watching YouTube videos on my dad's iPad (but only for 30 minutes on school nights or two hours at the weekend). I hope to have my own channel one day, where I will film my friends and me going off on all sorts of adventures. Look out for it. I also love writing, and that's how this story came about, as it's part of my diary of all events that have happened - good and bad.

## Chapter Four

# BAMZ AND THE CLUB

**Our** **group is** known as BAMZ. B is for Billy, A for Adam, M for Milly and Z for Zack. We have our own club, and we go on adventures, explore and help solve problems.

We have our meetings in the back of my garden, in our old garden shed. Dad used to keep all his tools in there, but as he doesn't need it any longer, he helped

us convert it into our very own club. He even stuck a sign on it for us, which we painted.  It's great!! We have a secret knock, to keep out adults and anyone else who's not in the club. We also have a secret handshake too, and sometimes, we even speak our very own BAMZ language, which we made up, but I can only tell you about that later.

In our club, we have some very important items. Without them, we could not do our work.

 This is a magnifying glass. I bought it in a garage sale for 50p and it's super! It lets me see tiny things in a big, big way.

This is a camera. You know the one I mentioned earlier? It's Milly's. Her dad got it for her because she came first in the swimming competition. It's cool. You take a picture, and it prints straight away. Like I said, it's sooo cool. I don't like the colour though. It's purple, which is my least favourite colour. Ugh!!

 This is a catapult - we made it from a broken branch and some elastic. We use it for secret missions, which I can't tell you about right now, but you'll find out soon.

OK, so now you know where our club is and you know some of the things we use in the club, but do you know what we do? OK, well first let me tell you about the secret.

## Chapter Five

# *THE SECRET*

**So,** **I've already** told you about my friends and me, and more importantly, you know about BAMZ. However, there is one very very big, important, ginormous, incredible, bigger than an elephant, no, forget about the elephant - it's bigger than the moon! It's even bigger than my Aunty Jasmine, and my dad says it would probably take a year to go around Aunty

Jas. It's **BIIIIIG**. It's **HUGE**. It's a **VERY, VERY, VERY** big **SECRET**.

Now, nobody knows - OK? Absolutely no one. So you have to promise that you won't tell anyone. Do you promise? I mean it. No one can know. Not your mum, not your dad, not your sister or your baby brother. Not even your friend, or your cat, dog, pet fish or even your kangaroo. Promise? Do you?

OK. Come closer. Come very close. So close that your nose touches this page and I can whisper in your ear. Ready? No, you have to tell me that you are ready. **READDDDYY?!!** OK!! So the secret is that we see *real* animals. No...no...I *know* we can all see real animals, but I bet you've never seen one talk. They are very shy, so they don't talk to many people. When you are asleep or walking in the park, and when they know you are not watching, they come out, behave, and talk just like you and me! Some animals are our friends, and some are not. Some are very rude. I will tell you more about them later. First, let me tell you how it all began and what happened next.

## Chapter Six

# THE DISCOVERY

**One** **afternoon after** school, I was helping my dad in the garden. He wanted me to help him plant some tulips that Mum really liked. We were just getting started when Dad went inside because he had received a phone call, leaving me to do some digging so that we could plant the flowers when he came back out.

He was gone for quite some time. As I was just about to dig the last hole, I could hear the faint sound of a conversation, coming just from the bush in the corner. I assumed it was from a radio or a mobile phone that somebody may have left in the garden.

"I think you look very pretty today," I heard.

"Oh thank you so much," the other voice said giggling.

I quickly crawled to the bush and could hear the conversation clearly. I pulled the leaves apart and there staring back at me, were two mice looking quite surprised. They didn't run like most mice would. They just stood there on their two back legs! It was strange. I felt silly thinking that it had been the mice who had been talking, and looked around for anywhere else that the sounds may have come from. However, I couldn't see anything, so I turned around to get back to my digging.

Then all of a sudden, a faint 'Hello' came from behind me. I quickly turned back to see the mice were waving at me. What??! The mice were waving!!!

26

"Hello!" One mouse said. I was shocked and fell back.

"Oh, please don't be alarmed," the other mouse spoke. "It's nice to finally meet you, Adam."

They knew my name! I couldn't speak. I didn't know what to say.

I finally replied back with a soft 'H..h.hello'. I was really surprised.

"Who are you? And what are you doing here?" I asked.

I learnt that the mice were called Bill and Jill. They had been living in my garden for quite some time and knew my name because mum and dad seemed to shout it quite often. They also knew of the other BAMZ members who they wanted to meet.

I couldn't quite believe it. I wanted to tell the others straight away, but I also wanted to keep Bill and Jill a secret for now. For about a week, I sneaked into the garden to talk to them, bringing them small pieces of cheese, which they really liked. One day when I visited them, I noticed Jill had a little bandage on her tail and Bill had a tiny cut on his cheek. They told me it was nothing, just an accident. I couldn't help thinking that there was more to it.

## Chapter Seven

# BAMZ CLUB FRIDAY

**It was Friday afternoon,** and we had just finished school. It was also the day we had our secret meeting at the BAMZ Club. Our parents let us stay out later on a Friday. A week had passed since I had met Bill and Jill and decided that I would tell the others about them this evening.

As Milly was the first to arrive, I told her first, as I just couldn't wait any longer. I explained how I came across the mice and how they were living in my garden. Milly thought I was joking and started laughing. She had her camera hanging around her neck. Her big brown eyes just stared at me as she stood with her arms folded, shaking her head.

"Why don't you believe me?" I asked, feeling very annoyed.

"Because mice don't talk Adam!" Milly responded. She thought I was making it up.

"Well, these ones do," I said seriously.

"Prove it!" she challenged me.

"Fine! We'll go out to the garden so you can see the mice for yourself," I suggested. I was getting excited.

"But we have to wait for Zack and Billy," Milly said. "They'll be here soon for our meeting."

"Well, why don't I go out to the garden and take a photo for you?" I was very impatient. I just couldn't wait. "Can I borrow your camera?"

"You didn't say the magic word!" Milly sighed. See, isn't she **SOOOO** annoying?

"Pleeease!?" I begged.

Milly rolled her eyes and handed me her camera, whilst she waited for Zack and Billy in the club. I ran out to the bush and called for Bill and Jill.

"Oh it's Adam!" Jill squealed, appearing from out of the bushes. "It's always a delight having you pay us a visit."

"Adam!" Bill clapped. "Good to see you, young man!"

I couldn't stay for long, so I explained how I had promised Milly a photo, and that the others would be visiting them soon.

"Ooo marvellous!" Bill said excitedly, clapping his paws. "We can't wait."

After asking for their permission, I took a photo of Bill and Jill, who both posed proudly in front of the camera. I then hurried back to the club to find Zack and Billy had arrived. Billy had his BAMZ T-shirt on.

"Milly told us about the mice," Zack said excitedly. "We can't wait to meet them! It could be a new discovery. We could put them up on your YouTube channel when it's ready. We could be famous!"

"You mean you actually believe him?" Milly looked surprised.

"Yes," replied Zack. "Why wouldn't we?!"

"I do too," said Billy.

"See, I told you!" I was pleased that at least Billy and Zack believed me, but also annoyed at Milly. "But Milly it wasn't your secret to tell."

"It's only a secret if it was true!" Milly snapped.

I showed her the picture I had taken using her camera. It showed Bill and Jill standing next to each other.

"Look, they're arguing," I explained. Bill and Jill had in fact been arguing about where they should stand for the picture.

"That doesn't prove they can talk! I can't hear *anything*." Milly frowned looking at the photo closely.

"Because it's a photo, silly!" I replied.

"They do look like they are talking." Billy added, putting the photo close to his ear, as if he could hear them.

"But animals don't talk, do they?" Milly grabbed the photo from Billy.

"They do," Billy squealed excitedly. "What about Winnie the Pooh and Peter Rabbit?"

"But they're not real!" she replied. I could see that Milly needed some convincing. "OK, let's go and see these *talking* mice then!"

We did our secret BAMZ handshake and headed out into the garden. (I will teach you the handshake later).

## Chapter Eight

# BILL AND JILL

**It was very quiet** in the garden. It was getting close to dark. Zack switched on the BAMZ torch so that we could see where we were going. There was a long pathway to the end of the garden.

As we didn't want to startle the mice, we slowly walked along the path. I was incredibly excited as I couldn't wait for the rest of BAMZ to meet Bill and Jill. We were almost there when I accidentally stood on Billy's foot!

**"OOOOUUUUCCCCHHHHHHH!"** Billy yelled.

**"SHHH!!!!"** we all shushed at him. **"SHHHHHHHHHHH!!!"**

"But it hurt," he moaned quietly.

"Sorry Billy!" I whispered.

We carried on, slowly tiptoeing until we reached the end of the garden.

"Stop." I whispered "Hello! Bill and Jill are you there?" There was no answer.

"See, no mice," Milly smirked. "Now let's get back to the club."

"No, wait," I said trying to listen for the smallest sound.

"Wait?" Milly asked. "For how long?"

"I don't know," I replied.

"I'm hungry," moaned Billy.

"You are always hungry!" Milly sighed.

She was right. Billy is always hungry. He always keeps chocolate in his pocket that he can pull out and munch on. Just like he did that day. Billy pulled out a chocolate bar and the wrapper made a **CRUMPLE, CRUMPLE, CRUMPLE** noise. If Billy could live in a house made of chocolate, he probably would. He would have a chocolate bath with chocolate water. His bed would be made of chocolate. I bet he would want to be made of chocolate and wear chocolate clothes and have friends made of chocolate. Good thing we aren't made of chocolate, or he would eat us all.

"Are you going to share that?" I asked. I couldn't help myself, I love chocolate too.

"No!!!!" Billy was famous for never sharing, especially food.

"Sharing is caring," Milly told him, whispering.

Billy ignored us and gobbled up the entire chocolate bar. He was sooooo greedy that his belly stuck out like a bear. I think he eats too much.

Bill and Jill were nowhere in sight. *Come on Bill and Jill, where are you?*

Then, all of a sudden, Bill and Jill appeared.

"And there you go." I held my arm out, pointing at the mice. "Meet Bill and Jill."

"Oh cooooool," said Billy. He crouched down, looking at them like he had never seen mice before.

"'Hello Bill and Jill. I'm Billy. We have similar names." The mice stared back at him, without saying a word.

"Are you sure they can talk Adam?" asked Zack.

"Patience Zack," I sighed. "They're just shy."

Bill and Jill walked back, to sit on tiny chairs placed at a small table. I had found these in an old toy box we had in the garage. Bill had one leg on top of his other knee. He was sitting very much like my dad does when he reads the newspaper. Jill was sat on the edge of the chair with her legs crossed.

"Well, hello you lot," said Bill. "We've been waiting for you."

"Wow! You can talk," Milly said surprised. Her big eyes growing even bigger as she bent down in surprise. "How amazing!"

"I told you!" I said, pleased with myself.

"Would you all like to stay for tea?" asked Jill.

"Oh, no thank you," said Zack. "We've already had our tea."

"I'd like some tea," Billy shrugged.

"He's had his tea," Milly interrupted, pulling Billy by his arm, as we all knew Billy would gobble up the small amounts of food that the mice had. Bill and Jill sat eating the cheese that I had brought them. They were so kind, because they were going to share their tiny piece of cheese with us.

"See Billy, sharing is caring," I said.

Before Billy could help himself to their food, we said a quick goodbye to the mice

and pulled him back towards the club. I was sorry to have to leave so soon, but it was almost dark. Also, I knew we'd be seeing them again, and when we did, I knew Zack, Milly and Billy would have lots of questions for them.

When we got back to the BAMZ club, I grabbed the BAMZ book. The book is a secret, highly classified book about what has happened in the day, just for us, the members of BAMZ. I usually write in it, and this is what I wrote. I also included the photo I had taken earlier using Milly's camera.

## Friday evening 19th July 2019

BAMZ finally all met Bill and Jill two mice, who lived in my (Adam's) garden. Bill and Jill can talk and today they sat on their chairs just like people do. They were eating cheese. We hope to see them again very soon as we have lots of questions to ask them. This is our secret. This is the truth mice can talk. If you can't keep a secret, then stay out !!!

signed

BAMZ

## Chapter Nine

# BAMZ TO THE RESCUE

**On** **Sunday morning,** just after breakfast, I had to call on the members of BAMZ for a very serious matter that had happened the previous night. I sent a secret code through our group chat that we had on our very own website.

Milly's dad had kindly set up a website for us all, which we used to chat and share stories, pictures and stuff. It was the only way we could communicate - through the site, as we weren't allowed to have our own mobile phone yet. The code I used was SHHH, which meant Something Has Happened Here. As soon as any BAMZ member saw this, they knew they had to get to whoever had sent the message.

About 30 minutes later, Billy, Milly and Zack arrived. They came through the back door. Mum wasn't very happy, because she was scared that they would step on all her flowers. Mum loves growing flowers. There are loads of them and they are so colourful, they look like Skittles scattered in the garden. Lucky for them, they didn't step on any.

"Adam! Come on. We have to go," Billy said. He was excited and slightly out of breath as he wanted to know what SHHH was all about.

"He's not going anywhere until he has finished his breakfast," Mum said, feeding Jamal, who seemed to be feeding most of his face.

I gobbled up my breakfast and ran out with the others.

"What's going on?" Milly asked.

"Well, I've had a visit from Bill and Jill," I explained.

I told the others how Bill and Jill had crept into my room in the early morning, asking for help. They were being terrorised by two mice who lived in Lion Hill Park. These mice were bullies. Their names were Bory and Gory and they were bullying Bill and Jill. They were creeping into the garden at night and stealing their food, pulling Jill's ears, and putting Bill upside down when he was sleeping. So, Bill and Jill decided that enough was enough and decided to tell someone, that someone being BAMZ! Exactly what you should do, if you are bullied. Tell someone!

I was angry. I wanted to catch these mice and teach them that bullying would never be tolerated. Our school and Mum and Dad had taught us never to stand by bullying, but to stand up to it. Telling someone, such as a teacher, your parents or anyone who can help, was very important.

"We need a plan," Zack said.

"That's easy!!" I responded. "We wait here and catch them."

"Yessss!" Billy shouted excitedly. Billy only ever agreed with us. He never had any clever ideas of his own.

"No, no," Milly disagreed. "That will take too long. Come on, let's go and see Bill and Jill, and see if we can find out more about what's going on."

We stepped into the garden to visit the mice. Bill and Jill looked terribly upset and explained the incident again to the others. Everyone listened carefully about how two mice bullies had crept into the garden last night and had chased both Bill and Jill around the garden, scaring them. We also learnt that this wasn't the first time that the bullying had taken place. We asked them where we would find these bullies. Zack pulled out a map from his pocket and asked the mice to show him. Bill pointed at the forest in the park, which was about five minutes from my house. He and Jill had followed the mice one day after they had stolen their food.

"We go and find them here," Zack said, pointing at the cross that he had just marked on the map.

"Alright then. Come on, let's go," Milly commanded. We all headed to the park.

## Chapter Ten

# BORY AND GORY

**The park was** very quiet. It was Sunday morning and there were only a few people around, walking their dogs or running. Zack led us to the forest and started following the map. I knew the forest well. I came here with Mum, Dad and Jamal sometimes. It wasn't that big for a forest, but it did have lots of trees.

"So, what are we looking for, Zack?" I asked.

"You'll see. Come on!" he looked at the map, then started walking faster down a trail as we followed behind.

Billy ran after us. "I can't keep up. Slow down."

Milly and I managed to catch up with Zack. We stood in front of an enormous tree. Zack was standing there appearing deep in thought. Billy came running up to us, catching his breath.

"So ...so ....what are we doing here?" Billy gasped for air.

Milly shushed him quietly and pointed at the hole in the tree. There were words carved just above: *B&G rule*. Just then, two mice appeared out of the hole. They looked quite shy.

"Don't be scared of us," whispered Billy as he approached the hole. The mice stood staring at Billy, who slowly walked up to them, covering them from sight.

"We just want to talk," Billy continued. There was silence and Billy just stood there. I was just about to tell him to move, when all of a sudden, he cried out.

"Ouch!!!" Billy screamed. He leapt away from the hole and grabbed his nose.

"What's wrong, Billy?" asked Zack.

"What happened?" I called.

"Ouch!!!!" he screamed again. **"OUUUUUCCCCCH!!!"**

"Whaaat?" I shouted.

"They hit me!" he screamed.

Billy was right. Before we could do anything, a small stone hurtled past me and fell on the ground. Then another, and another. Milly, Zack, and I moved quickly as a big heap of stones came flying our way. Ouch! Even though the stones were small, they still stung. Wow, the mice were really throwing stones at us.

"What's going on, Adam?" Billy shouted.

"I told you, Bill and Jill need our help," I explained, whilst swaying one way then the other, as I tried to dodge the stones.

"From these bullies!" Milly yelled.

Bory and Gory were a pain and kept on throwing stones at us. Zack and I managed to each grab a branch off the ground to bat the stones away. Soon they got tired and stopped. That is when Milly slowly approached the mice.

"Well, hello Bory and Gory," Milly said, with arms folded. Bory and Gory looked at each other and paused for a moment. "Oh don't look surprised, we know who you are and that you are big bullies!"

"But they're not really that big," whispered Billy.

Milly ignored Billy.

"No one likes bullies!" she carried on. "And do you know what happens to them?"

"They become rulers of the world." Bory laughed, or was it Gory? Finally the mice had spoke.

"No, they don't!" Milly said.

"Well, you are just a big girly liar who knows nothing," Gory replied.

Milly looked cross, but said nothing.

"And you two are just little bullies!" Billy shouted.

"You look like you are going to cry." The bullies laughed again.

"No, I'm not. You two don't scare me!" Billy answered back.

"I bet we do," they cackled. "Cry baby!! Boo hoo hoo!"

"You're not funny, you know!" I shouted.

"We are!!" They shouted back.

The mice weren't scared, and it was quite clear from what they said, that they were indeed bullies. The mouse that I assumed was Bory, was round and plump. Gory was skinny and taller than Bory. They both stood there looking mean. I just wanted to pick them up by their tails and tell them to stop. But I didn't. Instead, we decided we needed a plan.

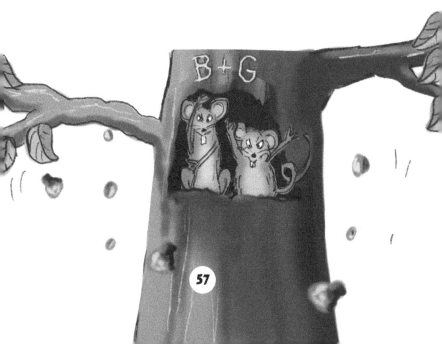

## Chapter Eleven

# THE PLAN

**After** **much discussion,** we decided that the best plan was to walk away. Bory and Gory started shouting behind us, calling us losers, but we ignored them, although Billy wanted to shout back. We found a small area in the park with a flat tree trunk and used it as a table. Zack rolled out a piece of paper.

"Right, members of BAMZ," he said. Zack always liked to take charge when it came to plans. He was quite good at it. "We need to plan how we are going to stop them."

"Stop them from what?" asked Billy.

"Stop being bullies Billy," I sighed. "Pay attention!"

"Well, we could always call them names back." Billy suggested. "Bory and Gory can be Boring and Grory."

"No, we can't do that," Milly said. "Because that would mean we are being just like them."

"Milly is right," Zack said. "We need another way to stop them from bullying Bill and Jill. Let's think about this."

"Well, what do mice not like? Maybe we show them something that scares them or puts them off," I suggested.

"They don't like cats," Billy mumbled, whilst munching on a big bar of chocolate. Billy really did not understand that sharing was caring.

That was actually a good idea. Cats and mice never really got on. Cats were always chasing mice. But where would we find a cat? Then, I remembered that my Aunt Jasmine had a cat. He's called Squiggles and although he is a lazy cat, he is very quick at running away. I remember when Aunt Jasmine's neighbour's dog chased Squiggles around the block. Squiggles was soooooooo fast, the dog never caught him.

"I can bring my Aunt Jasmine's cat if

you want. That might just stop them from being bullies"

"Hmm, let me write that idea down." Zack wrote it down on the piece of paper.

"Or if that doesn't work, how about we just tell them that if they bully Bill and Jill again, we will take them as far away from here as possible." I said.

"Boring Adam. So boring." That was Billy.

"Shut up Billy and eat your chocolate," I said annoyed.

Of course, the cat idea sounded the best so far, but if Squiggles was feeling lazy that day, he was never going to scare them. That's why we needed to come up with some more ideas.

"I have an idea!" Milly looked excited. Her eyes grew big and her smile even bigger. "Why don't we just ask them what they want?"

"What?" I looked at her, surprised. That wasn't an idea!

"I say we use a mousetrap," Billy said.

"No, that will hurt them and we don't want to do that," Zack spoke. "But I will write it down as a last resort."

None of these ideas were great, although, I thought bringing Aunt Jasmine's cat to scare them, might be our best option.

"OK, let's try and scare them with the cat first I guess," Zack said. Billy smiled and high-fived me.

## Chapter Twelve

# SQUIGGLES

**We left Bory** and Gory in the forest and went to set up the plan of bringing the cat into my garden, ready for when the bullies would strike again. Aunt Jasmine kindly lent me Squiggles when I told her we had a mouse problem in the garden. That evening, we put Squiggles in the corner of the garden, close to where Bill and Jill stayed. Squiggles had been half asleep but stirred when he saw

Bill and Jill.

"No Squiggles, Bill and Jill are our friends. It's the bullies, Bory and Gory you have to scare away. OK?" I told him.

Squiggles rolled his eyes and I'm sure I could hear a sigh. If Bill and Jill could speak, then I am sure Squiggles could too, but he was too lazy to talk. It was getting late, and the others had to get home, but we promised the mice that we'd be back first thing in the morning to check on them.

Early the next morning, after the others arrived, we hurried into the garden to check on Bill and Jill.  It was very quiet. Squiggles wasn't anywhere to be seen. Aunt Jasmine would be cross with me if I had lost him. Milly called out to Bill and Jill, but there was silence. I was feeling nervous. Where were they all?

"Wait!" whispered Milly.

We stopped and listened, but we couldn't hear anything besides Billy ruffling the leaves that had fallen on the grass. Then we heard it. A small cry for help coming from the corner of the garden.

Everyone slowly tiptoed to the corner trying not to make any sound. We could barely hear it, but someone was shouting for help! It sounded like Bill and Jill!

**"HEEELLLPPPP!"** cried Bill.

"Please help us!" shouted Jill.

We reached the corner, but they couldn't be seen. Then as I looked up, I spotted them. Bill and Jill were both hanging upside down, with their tails tied around the branch. Poor things. This was a cruel prank and Bory and Gory had a lot to answer for. But where was Squiggles and why had he not scared them off?

"Don't worry," shouted Billy as he struggled to climb the first branch of the tree. "I'll get you down."

"Be careful Billy," Zack shouted behind him.

Billy climbed up a thick tree branch so that he was directly above the mice. He slowly picked up Bill and untied his tail and then helped Jill. The mice looked relieved and grateful, and scurried down one branch, jumping onto another, until they were back on the grass.

**67**

"Thanks Billy," Jill was very grateful.

"We had no idea how long we would be here otherwise." said Bill.

We then listened to the account of the previous night, of how Bill and Jill had just gone to sleep, when Bory and Gory appeared. First, they were very quiet and then startled Bill and Jill by shouting "Boooo!". Bill and Jill started running and ran up the tree, but both Bory and Gory caught up with them, and that is when they managed to grab their tails and tie them around a branch.

"But I don't understand!" I was confused. "Where was Squiggles? I thought he was supposed to scare them away."

Bill and Jill shrugged their shoulders.

"They weren't scared of the cat," Bill explained. "In fact, they scared Squiggles away!"

**"WHAT???"** we all said at the same time.

Oh no. I was really in trouble with Aunt Jasmine now. I had no idea where to find Squiggles. Although I'd rather let him be lost as he had been useless, I was going to have to find him soon, else not only my aunt, but my whole family would probably ground me for life.

"But where did he run off to?" I panicked. "I'm in so much trouble."

"Oh he didn't go far," Jill explained, as she pointed further up at the tree above us. "He was so scared of Bory and Gory, that he has been up there since."

What a useless cat. We looked up and there he was, sleeping peacefully on a big branch. I was glad that I wasn't going to be in trouble with my aunt. We just had to get him down now, so I could take him back home. Billy, who loves climbing things as you know, crawled up the tree again, much to Squiggles disappointment. The cat screeched when he saw Billy, who quickly grabbed him and clambered back down the tree, with Squiggles firmly held in one arm.

"You didn't really help did you?" Milly stroked Squiggles like he deserved a reward. I am sure I noticed Squiggles squirm.

"Well, seems like we need to look at plan B," Zack suggested. "We still have a problem with the bullies."

Zack was right. We needed to look back at the plan. We said bye to Bill and Jill, promising them that we would solve the case of the bullies. I returned Squiggles back to Aunt Jasmine and then joined the others back at the forest.

## Chapter Thirteen

# MILLY'S PLAN

**Retu**rning to the tree where Bory and Gory lived, we saw them sitting outside, relaxing, like they had done nothing wrong. The bullies laughed when they saw us approaching.

"You thought you could scare us with a cat?" Bory mocked. "Cats don't scare us!"

"Yes, they do!" Billy snapped.

"Well, your silly cat didn't!" Gory sniggered.

Bory was right. Squiggles had failed to scare them, and instead ran up the tree when he saw Bory and Gory charge at him. If ever there was a useless cat, it was Squiggles. He is lazy and uncaring, and as Aunt Jasmine says, all he does is sleep all day. We now needed another plan of action to stop these bullies, else Bill and Jill would continue being bullied. It was time to look at Plan B. We walked away from the mice and Zack pulled out the list.

Zack crossed off number one as that plan had clearly failed. We then thought about our second option. Taking them far away seemed like a difficult job, especially as none of us are really allowed to go anywhere outside of the area we live in, so that only left two other options.

I personally didn't think setting a mouse trap was going to work. Also, it would be

1. ~~Scare them with a cat.~~
2. ~~Take them far away.~~
3. ~~Mouse trap.~~
4. Talk to them and ask them what they want.

cruel if it hurt them. The others agreed, although Billy suggested that we just catch their tail. How? I am not sure. So that left us with Milly's plan - talk to them and ask them what they want.

Milly seemed quite excited that the last plan of action was going to be what she had suggested. She was chosen to be the one to approach the mice, so with folded arms to show them that she was in charge, she marched up to Bory and Gory.

"I have a question for you two," Milly said sternly. "Why don't you like Bill and Jill?"

Bory and Gory stood there for a while, Gory leaning with his arm on Bory's shoulder.

"Because they smell," Gory said, and he and Bory started laughing.

"Stop joking," said Milly. "Tell us why you *really really* don't like them."

"Because they think they are better than us!" replied Gory.

"And they're just annoying!" added Bory.

"Yes! They have their own place in their garden. They have all these nice things," Gory added.

After more and more talking, we discovered the following about Bory and Gory, and why they thought it was OK to bully Bill and Jill. But just to say:

## "IT IS NEVER OK TO BE A BULLY!!"

## Chapter Fourteen

# ALL'S WELL THAT ENDS WELL

**It was quite easy** to solve the case of the bullies! If Bory and Gory had a better home, had good food and friends, then they would stop being mean - hmmm. That's not asking too much, right?

It wasn't that easy. First, they needed a home. Bill and Jill were living in my garden. Billy's was out of the question, as Samuel, the family dog, often played in the garden and who knows what he would do if he discovered Bory and Gory. That left Milly's and Zack's. Zack didn't really have a garden, only a balcony, which meant it would have to be Milly's. It had a lot of trees and bushes, so it would be fine. We had a quick meeting again by the tree trunk and agreed they would live in Milly's Garden.

Next, there was the food to sort out. Now, what do mice like to eat? Hmm, we decided it would be cheese and peanut butter, and that would be fine. Bill and Jill loved the scraps we gave them, so these food options should be good.

Then came friends. Now that was a difficult one. In order to have friends, you have to be nice and kind, as friends need to like you too. We wondered if Bill and Jill could be their friends and grow to like them. That is the secret formula - if you want to be liked and have lots of friends, you must be kind to everyone!

We approached the mice and read out the terms.

Both Bory and Gory laughed at our terms and made funny faces. Then, they heard about where they would live and the food they would eat.

"A home? In a garden?" Bory exclaimed. "We don't want to live in a garden!"

"But you just said you didn't like Bill and Jill because they did!" said Billy.

"And peanut butter - we want jelly with that!" demanded Gory.

"But mice don't eat jelly," Milly said.

"And we don't want to be friends with Bill and Jill!" said Bory.

"But you wanted more friends!?" Zack said.

"You can't be so picky!" I shouted. I was getting very annoyed with the mice. "This isn't the Hilton Hotel, you know!" That's what my dad always says.

Bory and Gory were selfish, mean, greedy and really not very nice. I wanted to pick them up by their tails and let them dangle in the air for a bit. That would serve them right!! But I didn't, because Zack said something very clever, which made them think.

"Well, you have two options," he said. "Take what we are offering you or stay here forever, where who only knows what might visit you."

"Big birds!" added Milly.

"A big rat!" I said.

"Or my Uncle Sam's pet snake Slither!" Billy shouted.

Bory and Gory sat there quietly, thinking of the options. Then they started whispering to each other. We couldn't hear what they were saying. After a few minutes, Bory spoke.

"Ok, we accept the offer. But you have to provide us with jelly *and* peanut butter."

"We will see what we can do," I said, trying not to look too pleased.

"As long as you promise never to be bullies again." Milly said sternly.

At last, Bory and Gory had agreed to stop bullying Bill and Jill. It was a win for us. BAMZ had saved the day - ***YAAAAAAAY!!!***

So we set up a home in Milly's garden. We used a big old tin box that we found. We didn't have any furniture, but we used small matchboxes and some toy bricks from Milly's brother's toys, as tables and chairs.

Bill and Jill also tried to make friends with Bory and Gory and invited them for a tea party. We provided the cheese and even some leftover jelly that Billy's mum had made. There was peanut butter too. We played some music, and they all had a dance too. It was fun and everyone had a great time!

That evening, after a long day of trying to set things up, we got together in our club. We had homemade chocolate cake that mum had made and glasses of strawberry flavoured milk. We let Billy have the biggest slice because of his love of chocolate. I then took out the BAMZ book and recorded the day's events, also adding the picture that Milly took of everyone.

Sunday 21st July 2019

We saved Bill and Jill from 2 bullies, Bory and Gory, who are also mice, Billy has a swollen nose from when the bullies pelted him with a small stone. Bory and Gory are our friends now and will not be bullying Bill and Jill anymore. Overall, it was a fun weekend. We learnt it is never OK to bully anyone. And if you are being bullied, it's important to tell someone. Let's see what the next adventure holds.

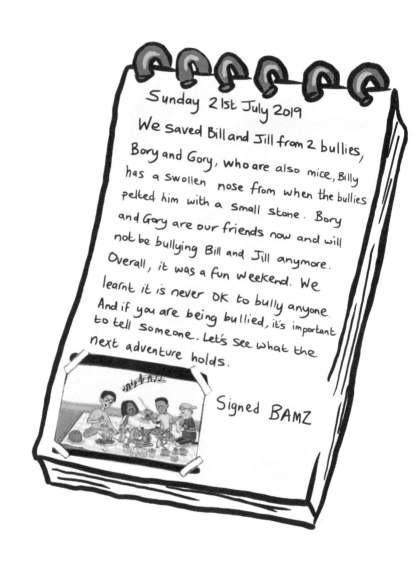

Signed BAMZ